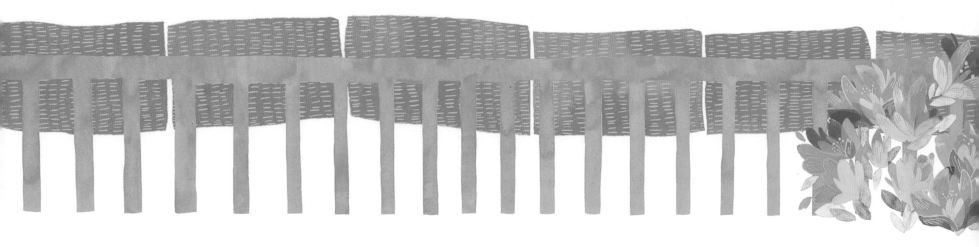

For everyone who lifts up a backpack and sets off.

And for Mabel,
who believed in this journey even before I did.

Katherine Tegen Books is an imprint of HarperCollins Publishers · To the Other Side · Copyright © 2023 by Erika Meza · All rights reserved Manufactured in Italy · No part of this book may be used or reproduced in any manner whatsoever without written permission except in the case of brief quotations embodied in critical articles and reviews. For information address HarperCollins Children's Books, a division of HarperCollins Publishers, 195 Broadway, New York, NY 10007 · www.harpercollinschildrens.com · Library of Congress Control Number: 2021041938 · ISBN 978-0-06-307316-6 · The artist used gouache, ink, POSCA markers, and Photoshop to create the illustrations for this book · Typography by Dana Fritts and Caitlin Stamper · 22 23 24 25 26 RTLO 10 9 8 7 6 5 4 3 2 1 ❖ First Edition

KA MEZA

TO

THE

OTHER

SIDE

KT KATHERINE TEGEN BOOKS
An Imprint of HarperCollins Publishers

"The rules of the game are simple,"
my sister said.

"Avoid the monsters."

"Don't get caught."

"And keep moving."

She promised the masks would hide us.
Make us fast. Make us brave.
It's like tag.
If the monsters catch you, you're out.

"We win the game when we cross the line."
Everyone was racing to see who could get there faster.

We walked. Caught rides. Or bused.

My sister would let me sit on her lap.
At times she complained I was too heavy.

On and on we went.
Sometimes with help.

Sometimes alone.

But always together.

On and on we waited.
Sometimes we played and
jumped and laughed.
And then we waited again.
I drew home in the dirt.
I drew us.
A line.
Ants slowly crossed it.

It's so, so hard to wait.

We thought hard of what
we might win.

"A home!"

"A really big
school!"

"A spotty dog!"

"A pair of
shiny red shoes."

My sister made me strong.

She smelled of home.

She kept me safe.

But this game was too long. Too tiring. Too hard.
I did NOT want to play anymore.

"¿Cuánto falta?" I asked her.
She squished my hand. "A bit longer!"

"Is this the finish line?"
"Shh!" she whispered. "Don't look back!"

"This isn't a game . . . is it?" I asked.

"No." My sister held me hard.
"I know you're scared," she said.
"But you're brave like a tiger.
I'm fast like a rabbit."

"And we are on our way home, together."

I slept harder than ever before.

Soon there were only a few of us left.

And finally, *finally*—I could see the border!

"We are almost there!"
My sister pulled me ahead.

But the game wasn't over yet.
There's always another line to cross.
And this line felt so very long.

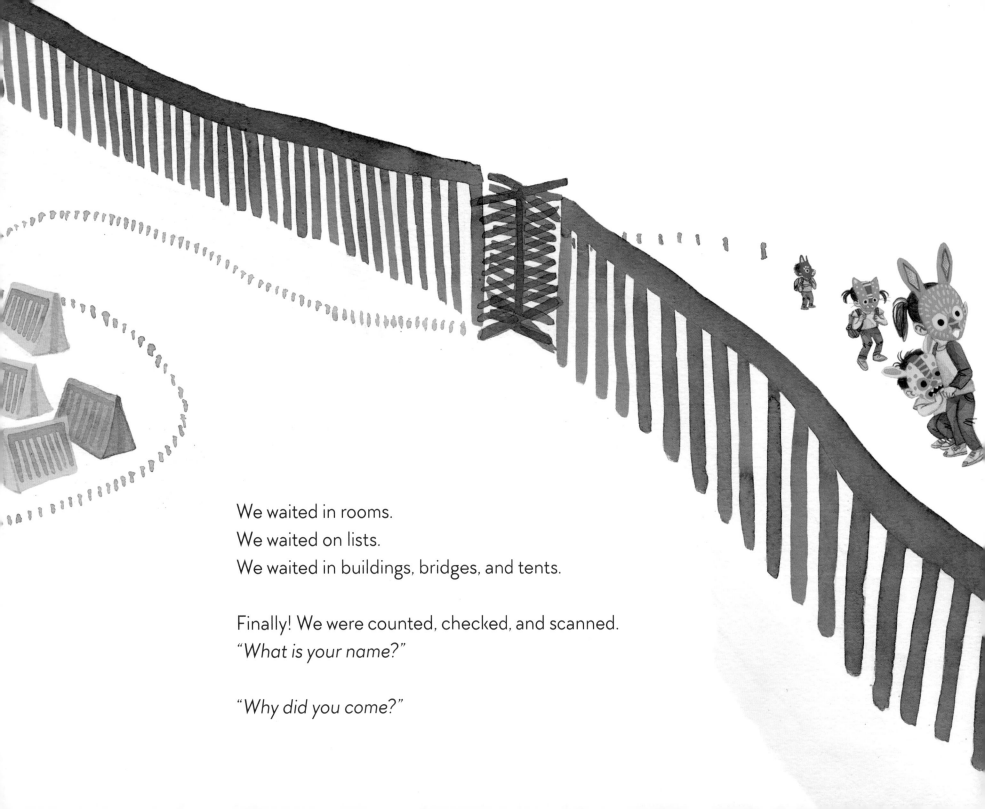

We waited in rooms.
We waited on lists.
We waited in buildings, bridges, and tents.

Finally! We were counted, checked, and scanned.
"What is your name?"

"Why did you come?"

"Speak clearly!" my sister whispered.
Her hand felt sweaty.
    She answered questions.

    And at last we were free to cross to
the other side.

But once we did . . .

...it didn't feel like we had won.

Not at first.

Not until I looked closer.

Now I have a new friend. He welcomed us into his home.

I drew a line on the ground and I told him . . .
"The rules of the game are simple."

AUTHOR'S NOTE

The act of migration was never anything new for my family or myself: by the time I am writing these lines, I am thirty-four years old and have moved thirty-five times for a total of seven different cities. I know what it's like to be stuck in a labyrinthine system, unable to explain yourself in a language you don't yet know. However, I've never known the shock or the horror of leaving everything you own, everyone you know, and then disappearing into the night, with hope—but not certitude—that you will find safety at the end of a dangerous and long journey. And yet, as you're reading these words, thousands of refugees across the world are doing just that: packing the bare essentials and praying to their god to let them reach their destination. I was already in the UK when I heard the cries of children asking in my mother tongue to be reunited with their families after the US separation policy was exposed in 2018. Many children had crossed the border through my hometown of Tijuana, and had suffered through the hurdles that my own country had laid on their path to stop them—or hurt them. And that is how the arduous road to build this book started.

Migrants and refugees are often portrayed as either heroes or villains; and yet, the children I was lucky to meet when working on this book were simply that: children. They liked pandas, dreamed of seeing a snowfall, wondered whom to gift a special doll to, and tried to help their parents with their younger siblings. Whatever their paths, whatever the monsters chasing them from their homes, they deserve to have the same choice I had: to cross an invisible line and, quite simply, be allowed to grow roots again, in a place of their choosing, where they finally feel safe.

Thank you to the families, young children, and Espacio Migrante for sharing your stories with me.